W9-DEH-314

Cuddle!

Written by
Beth Shoshan

Illustrated by
Jacqueline East

Albury Books

I'd cuddle a whale,
but I might be
too small,

I'd cuddle
a giraffe,
but I think
he's too tall.

I'd cuddle
a hedgehog
but, **ouch!**,
they're so spiky,

I'd cuddle a crocodile.

If I cuddled
a gorilla

I would end up much thinner,

If I cuddled a tiger
I'd end up as dinner.

I'd cuddle a skunk
but I think they're
too smelly,

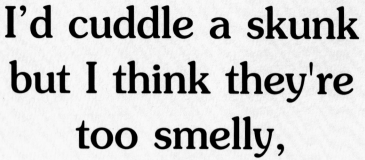

I'd cuddle a shark

but I'd be in his belly!

I'd cuddle
a python

way up high
in a tree

I'd cuddle
a hippo
who might
just
squash me.

Do you think
I can cuddle
my Teddy
instead?

For Uncle John
&
Aunty Sheila

J.E.

First published in 2006
by Meadowside Children's Books

This edition published by Albury Books
Albury Court, Albury, Thame, Oxfordshire,
OX9 2LP, United Kingdom
www.AlburyBooks.com

Illustrations © Jacqueline East 2006

The right of Jacqueline East to be identified
as the illustrator of this work has been
asserted by her in accordance with the Copyright,
Designs and Patents Act, 1988

A CIP catalogue record for this book
is available from the British Library

Printed in China

978-1-910571-22-4